DreamWorks

the BAD GUYS

THE BIGGEST, BADDEST FILL-IN BOOK EVER!

by Terrance Crawford

SCHOLASTIC INC.

ISBN 978-1-338-74570-2

10 9 8 7 6 5 4 3 2 1 22 23 24 25 26

Printed in the U.S.A. 40

First printing 2022

Book design by Jess Meltzer

Meet **THE BAD GUYS**. When you're born as *them*, you don't exactly win many popularity contests (though they might know someone who can fix one for ya!). But when those are the cards you've been dealt, you might as well play them. Yeah, they may be *bad*, but they're so *good* at it!

HOW TO PULL OFF A BIG SCORE:

1. GRAB A FRIEND, COHORT, OR CONFIDANTE AND A PENCIL (OR A PEN IF YOU'RE BRAVE!)
2. KNOW YOUR PARTS OF SPEECH—NOUNS, VERBS, ADVERBS, AND ADJECTIVES
3. ALWAYS HAVE AN EXIT PLAN (THIS ONE MAY ONLY APPLY TO ACTUAL HEISTS)

WOLF-THE MASTERMIND

ADJECTIVE ______________________

ADJECTIVE ______________________

TIME OF DAY ______________________

NOUN ______________________

LARGE ANIMAL ______________________

EXPENSIVE ITEM ______________________

PLACE ______________________

NOUN ______________________

NUMBER ______________________

PLURAL NOUN ______________________

ADVERB ______________________

ADJECTIVE ______________________

ADJECTIVE ______________________

ADJECTIVE ______________________

As ______ (adjective) as he is ______ (adjective), Wolf spends most of his ______ (time of day) plotting new ways for the Bad Guys to secure their Bad guys (noun). Like the time he convinced a/n ______ (large animal) to help him carry a/n ______ (expensive item) out of a ______ (place).

To be fair, he did promise a ______ (noun) and ______ (number) ______ (plural noun) for its troubles! Wolf is not to be taken ______ (adverb).

He is ______ (adjective), ______ (adjective), and dangerous!

Most importantly, he's so bad—*he's* ______ (adjective).

SNAKE–THE SAFECRACKER

Favrits this

ADJECTIVE ____________________

PERSON Snake ____________________

PERSON ____________________

PLACE ____________________

ADJECTIVE ____________________

PLACE ____________________

NOUN ____________________

UNIT OF TIME ____________________

BODY PART ____________________

NOUN ____________________

ADJECTIVE ____________________

PLURAL ANIMAL ____________________

ADJECTIVE ____________________

The ____________ counter to Wolf—the
(adjective)

____________ to Wolf's ____________—Snake
(person) (person)

is the best safecracker in ____________. Using
(place)

his ____________ body to navigate vents,
(adjective)

security systems, and ____________, Snake
(place)

can get in and out of any ____________ in
(noun)

____________! He can use his ____________ to
(unit of time) (body part)

smell ____________ around him, which
(noun)

makes him a/n ____________ heist partner,
(adjective)

as long as there are no ____________ around!
(plural animal)

Snake is much more ____________ than
(adjective)

Wolf but don't underestimate him!

TARANTULA-THE HACKER

NOUN ______

MACHINE ______

PLACE ______

VERB ______

LOCAL BUSINESS ______

NOUN ______

ADJECTIVE ______

NUMBER ______

PLURAL BODY PART ______

NUMBER ______

NOUN ______

NUMBER ______

VERB ______

Tarantula is a wiz on the ____________________.
(noun)

Every heist crew needs a hacker, someone who can turn off the ____________________ (machine) at the ____________________ (place) or ____________________ (verb) the security codes at the ____________________ (local business).

Tarantula may be a bit of a/n ____________________ (noun), and a little ____________________ (adjective)—but when you've got ____________________ (number) ____________________ (plural body part), you've got to have ____________________ (number) the times of ____________________ (noun)! She has gotten the crew out of over ____________________ (number) tough spots. Tarantula is one arachnid you can really ____________________ (verb) on.

SHARK—THE MASTER OF DISGUISE

ROYAL TITLE ______________________

NUMBER ______________________

NOUN ______________________

VERB ______________________

NUMBER ______________________

NOUN ______________________

CHARACTER ______________________

ADJECTIVE ______________________

WEBSITE ______________________

CHARACTER ______________________

ADJECTIVE ______________________

ADJECTIVE ______________________

VERB ______________________

TIP:
A royal title is a word like *king* or *queen*!

Shark—The ______________ of Disguise. Shark is
(royal title)

not just a/n ________-pound fish, he's a trained
(number)

costumer, ________________, and *actor*. Shark is
(noun)

always ready to ___________________ into a role.
(verb)

The shark of _______________ faces, his greatest
(number)

trick was stealing _____________________ while
(noun)

dressed as _________________. Though if you ask
(character)

him, the _________________________ day of his life
(adjective)

was when ___________________________ referred to
(website)

his performance of __________________________ as
(character)

"__________________________."
(adjective)

Aside from his skills as

an actor, Shark has a/n

____________________ heart
(adjective)

and is quick to

_________________.
(verb)

PIRANHA-THE SCRAPPER

NOUN ____________________

NOUN ____________________

ADJECTIVE ____________________

NOUN ____________________

VERB ____________________

ADJECTIVE ____________________

ADJECTIVE ____________________

ADJECTIVE ____________________

VERB ENDING IN -ING ____________________

ADJECTIVE ____________________

ADJECTIVE ____________________

ADVERB ____________________

VERB ____________________

VERB ____________________

NOUN ____________________

Piranha is . . . well, he's a bit of a/n

_______________ (noun). A _______________ (noun) with a fuse

as _______________ (adjective) as _______________ (noun), Piranha

is willing to _______________ (verb) anyone.

He's _______________ (adjective), he's _______________ (adjective),

and . . . who are we kidding? He's _______________ (adjective).

Almost as handy as his _______________ (verb ending in -ing) skills

is his _______________ (adjective) gas, always

_______________ (adjective) for a/n _______________ (adverb) escape!

Just because he's small doesn't mean that

anyone should _______________ (verb) this

feisty fish! Piranha won't

hesitate to take a/n

_______________ (verb) out of

_______________ (noun),

so watch out!

THE CHIEF OF POLICE

NOUN ______________________________

FOOD ______________________________

ADJECTIVE ______________________________

TITLE ______________________________

NOUN ______________________________

AMOUNT OF TIME ______________________________

VERB ______________________________

AMOUNT OF TIME ______________________________

ADJECTIVE ______________________________

VERB ENDING IN -ING ______________________________

VERB ENDING IN -ED ______________________________

NOUN ______________________________

TIP:
A title can be anything from *Chief* to *Doctor*!

Any ____________ (noun) worth their ____________ (food) will tell you that a Bad Guy is only as ____________ (adjective) as their Good Guy. That's where the police ____________ (title) comes in. She's been on the ____________ (noun) for ____________ (amount of time), and on the ____________ (verb) for Wolf and the Bad Guys for ____________ (amount of time), ever since their ____________ (adjective) adventure, when she almost put them away for Reckless ____________ (verb ending in -ing). She hasn't ____________ (verb ending in -ed) them yet, but it's only a matter of ____________ (noun) . . .

WANTED

WOLF

WANTE

SNAK

BAD GUYS ON WHEELS

ADJECTIVE ____________________

VEHICLE ____________________

ADJECTIVE ____________________

ADJECTIVE ____________________

VEHICLE ____________________

VERB ENDING IN -ED ____________________

NOUN ____________________

ADJECTIVE ____________________

ADJECTIVE ____________________

ADJECTIVE ____________________

FAVORITE DRINK ____________________

VERB ____________________

VEHICLE ____________________

No crew would be ______________ (adjective) without a getaway ______________ (vehicle), but the Bad Guy mobile is ______________ (adjective). Not just a/n ______________ (adjective) ______________ (vehicle) the Bad Guy mobile is ______________ (verb ending in -ed) with all sorts of ______________ (noun), including ______________ (adjective) tires, ______________ (adjective) steering wheel, and an extra special ______________ (adjective) cup holder for Wolf's ______________ (favorite drink). I would be afraid for anyone who ______________ (verb) with Wolf's getaway ______________ (vehicle). He loves his ride!

THE BANK JOB

DAY OF THE WEEK ______________

VERB ______________

PLACE ______________

NOUN ______________

SOUND ______________

ADJECTIVE ______________

DRINK ______________

ADJECTIVE ______________

VERB ______________

NOUN ______________

VERB ENDING IN -ED ______________

VERB ENDING IN -ING ______________

VERB ENDING IN -ED ______________

NOUN ______________

ADJECTIVE ______________

NOUN ______________

VERB ENDING IN -ED ______________

VERB ______________

TIP:
A sound can be something like *crash* or *rustling*.

It's just a normal ______________ (day of the week). Wolf and Snake ______________ (verb) in a/n ______________ (place), taking in the smell of the ______________ (noun) and the sound of ______________ (sound). Snake sips a/n ______________ (adjective) ______________ (drink). "You know one ______________ (adjective) thing about this place?" asked Wolf. "You never have to ______________ (verb) for a/n ______________ (noun)." "Isn't that every place?" Snake ______________ (verb ending in -ed), ______________ (verb ending in -ing) as they ______________ (verb ending in -ed) and made their way toward the ______________ (noun), past a group of ______________ (adjective) ______________ (noun) ______________ (verb ending in -ed) under a table. "We've got to ______________ (verb) you to decaf," said Wolf.

THE THRILL OF THE CHASE

NOUN ______________________

LIQUID ______________________

NOUN ______________________

PLURAL VEHICLE ______________________

NOUN ______________________

COLOR ______________________

COLOR ______________________

VERB ______________________

NOUN ______________________

SOUND EFFECT ______________________

COLOR ______________________

VERB ______________________

PLURAL NOUN ______________________

PLURAL NOUN ______________________

VEHICLE ______________________

VERB ENDING IN -ED ______________________

VERB ENDING IN -ING ______________________

VERB ENDING IN -ING ______________________

NOUN ______________________

VERB ENDING IN -ED ______________________

TIP: A sound effect is something like *BLAM* or *KABOOM*!

The ________ (noun) in your hair, the ________ (liquid) coursing through your veins. It was no wonder the chase was Wolf's favorite part of a/n ____________ (noun). The police's ______________________ (plural vehicle) were closing in around the Bad Guys, a/n __________ (noun) of ____________ (color) and ____________ (color) lights. But then, Tarantula ________________ (verb) something on her ____________ (noun) and . . . ____________ (sound effect)! All of the streetlights turn ____________ (color) and the Bad Guys ____________ (verb) away! "I'm going to put you away for so long your ____________ (plural noun) will have ____________ (plural noun)!" shouted the police chief as her ________________ (vehicle) ________________ (verb ending in -ed) to a halt. "Keep ________________ (verb ending in -ing)! One of these days your ________________ (verb ending in -ing) is gonna run out!" the police chief said as she threw her ________________________ (noun) to the ground and ________________ (verb ending in -ed) on it. The Bad Guys did it again!

HOME SWEET HOME

NOUN ______________________

ADJECTIVE ______________________

VERB ______________________

ARTICLE OF CLOTHING ______________________

SOMETHING EXPENSIVE ______________________

VERB ______________________

ADJECTIVE ______________________

VERB ______________________

PREPOSITION ______________________

PLACE ______________________

VERB ______________________

ADJECTIVE ______________________

NOUN ______________________

ADVERB ______________________

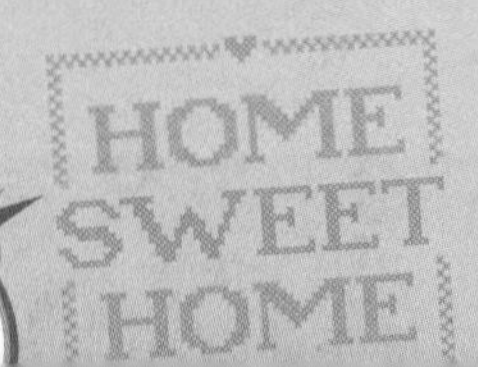

Sure, the life of a ______ (noun) is ______ (adjective),

but now and then, you've got to come home.

A place to ______ (verb) your ______ (article of clothing).

Plus, what's the point of stealing

______ (something expensive) if you don't have anywhere

to ______ (verb) it? The Bad Guys' lair

isn't exactly ______ (adjective) to get

to. In order to get there, they have to

______ (verb) ______ (preposition) the

______ (place) and ______ (verb) through a/n

______ (adjective) tunnel.

If you're like us, you can't

allow just any ______ (noun) to

waltz right into your

______ (adverb) hideout.

GOOD ST

BAD GUY WAY

THE GRAND TOUR

ADJECTIVE ______________________

PLACE ______________________

EXPENSIVE ITEM ______________________

PLACE ______________________

YEAR ______________________

ADJECTIVE ______________________

CELEBRITY ______________________

PERSON ______________________

FAVORITE MEAL ______________________

ADJECTIVE ______________________

ADJECTIVE ______________________

How are the most ____________________ (adjective) criminals in the city living? Take a look for yourself.

Where else in ____________________ (place) could you find a/n ____________________ (expensive item) missing from ____________________ (place) since ____________________ (year), or the ____________________ (adjective) ____________________ (celebrity) tapes, or ____________________ (person)'s recipe for ____________________ (favorite meal)?

The Bad Guys may be ____________________ (adjective), but they are ____________________ (adjective) at what they do!

LAIR CAKE

PLACE ____________________

SPECIAL OCCASION ____________________

PLURAL NOUN ____________________

COLOR ____________________

COLOR ____________________

NOUN ____________________

NOUN ____________________

FOOD ____________________

SAME SPECIAL OCCASION ____________________

ADJECTIVE ____________________

FAVORITE SONG ____________________

NOUN ____________________

ADJECTIVE ____________________

VERB ENDING IN -ED ____________________

NOUN ____________________

VERB ENDING IN -ING ____________________

TIP:
A special occasion is something like an *anniversary* or *birthday*!

Today, the ____________________ is decorated for
(place)

____________________ . The ____________________ are
(special occasion) (plural noun)

turned all the way up, ____________________ and
(color)

____________________ banners hang from the
(color)

____________________ , there is ____________________ on
(noun) (noun)

the ceiling, and Wolf ordered ____________________ .
(food)

In honor of ____________________ , Piranha
(same special occasion)

even sings a/n ____________________ rendition
(adjective)

of ____________________ . It's no secret
(favorite song)

that Piranha has the voice of a/n ____________________ .
(noun)

Most of the Bad Guys look pretty ____________________ .
(adjective)

"Wait!" ____________________ Wolf, looking toward
(verb ending in -ed)

the ____________________ . "They're
(noun)

____________________ about us!"
(verb ending in -ing)

REPORTING LIVE

NUMBER ______________________

ADJECTIVE ______________________

NOUN ______________________

TIME OF DAY ______________________

ADJECTIVE ______________________

VEHICLE ______________________

ADJECTIVE ______________________

NOUN ______________________

TIME OF DAY ______________________

"JUNK" FOOD ______________________

VEGETABLE ______________________

TIP:
"Junk" food is anything from *chips* to *chocolate*.

"Hello, I'm Tiffany Fluffit, Channel

__________ (number) News. Today, the Bad Guys pulled

off their most __________ (adjective) __________ (noun) yet.

Beginning at __________ (time of day), the

__________ (adjective) lawbreakers used

a/n __________ (vehicle) to facilitate

their escape. Proving that they are the most

__________ (adjective) __________ (noun) of

our time. More on this at __________ (time of day).

But first . . . is __________ ("junk" food) the new

__________ (vegetable)? Stay tuned for more."

INTERVIEW WITH A GOVERNOR

NOUN ____________________

VERB ____________________

VERB ____________________

ADJECTIVE ____________________

ADJECTIVE ____________________

ADJECTIVE ____________________

NOUN ____________________

VERB ____________________

ADJECTIVE ____________________

NOUN ____________________

AMOUNT OF TIME ____________________

ADJECTIVE ____________________

VERB ENDING IN -S ____________________

ADJECTIVE ____________________

Governor Diane Foxington takes the ____________ (noun) from Tiffany and begins to ____________ (verb) into it. "Let's ____________ (verb) the Bad Guys and focus on more ____________ (adjective) things! And what could be more ____________ (adjective) than the Annual ____________ (adjective) ____________ (noun) Awards? Where I will ____________ (verb) the ____________ (adjective) ____________ (noun) trophy to this ____________ (amount of time)'s ____________ (adjective) citizen!"

Wolf ____________ (verb ending in -s) the television. "She thinks we're ____________ (adjective)? I can't believe I voted for her!"

THE BIG SCORE

VERB ____________________

ADJECTIVE ____________________

ADJECTIVE ____________________

ADJECTIVE ____________________

NOUN ____________________

NOUN ____________________

ADJECTIVE ____________________

PLURAL NOUN ____________________

ADJECTIVE ____________________

VERB ENDING IN -ING ____________________

PLACE ____________________

NUMBER ____________________

UNIT OF TIME ____________________

VERB ____________________

"Alright, guys! Who is up for one more _______ ?
(verb)

A/n _______________ one, to prove we're
(adjective)

not _______________ . What about . . . the
(adjective)

_______________ _______________ trophy?
(adjective) (noun)

It's made of solid _______________ with two
(noun)

_______________ _______________ for eyes.
(adjective) (plural noun)

And the _______________ part? They just
(adjective)

said on TV that they're _______________ at
(verb ending in -ing)

the _______________ in less than
(place)

_______ _______________ ."
(number) (unit of time)

Can the Bad Guys really

_______________ this one off?
(verb)

THIS TIME, IT'S PERSONAL

BODY PART ______________________

NOUN ______________________

VERB ______________________

ADJECTIVE ______________________

NOUN ______________________

VERB ENDING IN -ED ______________________

FRIEND NAME ______________________

FRIEND NAME ______________________

VERB ______________________

NOUN ______________________

BODY PART ______________________

VERB ______________________

NOUN ______________________

ADJECTIVE ______________________

Tarantula raises her ________________ (body part). "I hate to be a/n ____________ (noun), but everyone who has tried to ________ (verb) the ______________ (adjective) ____________ (noun) trophy has been ____________________ (verb ending in -ed)! ____________________ (friend name), ____________________ (friend name), Lucky Jim, The Crimson Paw . . ." "Exactly!" said Wolf. "What better way to stick it to Foxington than to ______________ (verb) the ____________________________ (noun) right from under her ____________________________ (body part)? If we pull this off, we ____________________ (verb) our __________________ (noun) as the ____________________________________ (adjective) criminals of all time!"

THE BIG PLAN—STEP ONE

AMOUNT OF TIME ______________________________

PLACE ______________________________

ADJECTIVE ______________________________

NOUN ______________________________

DIRECTION ______________________________

ADJECTIVE ______________________________

NOUN ______________________________

VERB ______________________________

FAMOUS PERSON ______________________________

NOUN ______________________________

JOB ______________________________

NOUN ______________________________

COLOR ______________________________

ITEM OF CLOTHING ______________________________

"Here's the plan. Just like every

_______________, the ceremony will be held at
(amount of time)

__________, where the _________ _________ trophy
(place) (adjective) (noun)

will be positioned just _______________ of
(direction)

the _________________ _________________.
(adjective) (noun)

To get there, we need to _______________ past
(verb)

three levels of security. For step one, we'll

need to *blend in*. Shark will be disguised as

_________________, Tarantula as a/n
(famous person)

____________________, Snake as
(noun)

a/n _____________ with a/n
(job)

___________ and Piranha
(noun)

will have to wear a

_______ _____________,"
(color) (item of clothing)

Wolf said.

MEET THE PROFESSOR

VEHICLE ____________________

PLACE ____________________

PLURAL VERB ____________________

FAMOUS PERSON ____________________

FAMOUS PERSON ____________________

ADJECTIVE ____________________

NOUN ____________________

VERB ENDING IN -ED ____________________

AMOUNT OF TIME ____________________

VERB ENDING IN -ED ____________________

ADJECTIVE ____________________

NUMBER ____________________

FAVORITE ANIMAL ____________________

NOUN ____________________

FAMOUS PERSON ____________________

NOUN ____________________

NOUN ____________________

ADJECTIVE ____________________

VERB ____________________

A/n ______________ pulls up to ______________ and
(vehicle) (place)

out __________________ Professor Marmalade—a
(plural verb)

mixture of ______________________________ and
(famous person)

______________________, and the recipient of the
(famous person)

___________________ __________________ trophy.
(adjective) (noun)

He is immediately __________________________ by
(verb ending in -ed)

Tiffany Fluffit. "Professor! In the last

________________, you have ________________ the
(amount of time) (verb ending in -ed)

_________________ and saved ________________ of
(adjective) (number)

__________________________. Some have described
(favorite animal)

your _________________________ as second only to
(noun)

_________________________." Marmalade let out a/n
(famous person)

_______________________. "Oh, I think we can all
(noun)

agree that there is a/n ______________________ of
(noun)

________________________ inside all of us, just
(adjective)

waiting to _____________________!"
(verb)

THE BIG PLAN-STEP TWO

NUMBER ____________________

ADJECTIVE ____________________

VERB ENDING IN -ED ____________________

NOUN ____________________

VERB ENDING IN -ED ____________________

BODY PART ____________________

ADJECTIVE ____________________

NOUN ____________________

NOUN ____________________

VERB ____________________

VERB ENDING IN -ED ____________________

PLURAL NOUN ____________________

VERB ____________________

VERB ____________________

Wolf launched into the next phase of his big plan. "Once we're inside, there are going to be ____________ (number) ____________ (adjective) doors. These doors can only be ____________ (verb ending in -ed) by a/n ____________ (noun) that is ____________ (verb ending in -ed) at all times by the Chief of Police. The other doors have ____________ (body part) scanners so ____________ (adjective) that they could tell a/n ____________ (noun) from a/n ____________ (noun). If we get past that, we ____________ (verb) into the doors that are ____________ (verb ending in -ed) by ____________ (plural noun) trained to ____________ (verb) first and ____________ (verb) later."

THE BIG PLAN– STEP THREE

VERB ______________________

NOUN ______________________

NOUN ______________________

VERB ______________________

NOUN ______________________

JOB ______________________

VERB ______________________

VERB ______________________

VERB ______________________

PLURAL VERB ______________________

PLURAL VERB ______________________

ADJECTIVE ______________________

VERB ______________________

VERB ENDING IN -ING ______________________

"Do your thing, Shark!" Wolf ______ (verb) into his ______ (noun). Shark, dressed as a/n ______ (noun), begins to ______ (verb). "I'm having a/n ______ (noun)! Is there a/n ______ (job) or perhaps several guards who could ______ (verb) their posts and ______ (verb) me!" It works! As the guards ______ (verb), Piranha ______ (plural verb) Wolf to the Security Room and ______ (plural verb) him inside using a/n ______ (adjective) keycard! The Bad Guys ______ (verb) as Marmalade gives his speech. They are so close to ______ (verb ending in -ing) their mission!

SPEAK THE SPEECH

VERB ENDING IN -ED ____________________

UNIT OF TIME ____________________

VERB ENDING IN -ED ____________________

ADVERB ____________________

NOUN ____________________

ADJECTIVE ____________________

SAME NOUN ____________________

NOUN ____________________

NOUN ____________________

NOUN ____________________

PLACE ____________________

NOUN ____________________

ADJECTIVE ____________________

Governor Foxington ______________________ down
(verb ending in -ed)

into the microphone. "Last _______________ we
(unit of time)

_________________ our _______________ test
(verb ending in -ed) (adverb)

when a/n ____________________ crashed into our
(noun)

_____________ city. That _____________ didn't
(adjective) (same noun)

just make a hole in our ____________________.
(noun)

It made a hole in our ____________________.
(noun)

But now the ____________________ in
(noun)

_____________________ will forever
(place)

serve as a symbol of how there is

_______________, even in the
(noun)

____________ places."
(adjective)

A SPARK OF GOODNESS

NOUN ______________________

ADJECTIVE ______________________

ADJECTIVE ______________________

NOUN ______________________

NOUN ______________________

VERB ______________________

NOUN ______________________

VERB ______________________

VERB ______________________

VERB ENDING IN -S ______________________

VERB ENDING IN -S ______________________

BODY PART ______________________

VERB ______________________

NOUN ______________________

VERB ENDING IN -S ______________________

Wolf is in the middle of his ______________ when
(noun)

he comes up behind a very ______________-looking
(adjective)

______________ woman, ______________ spilling
(adjective) (noun)

out of her ______________. Right as
(noun)

Wolf goes to ______________ the lady's ______________,
(verb) (noun)

she ______________ and starts to
(verb)

______________ down the stairs! Wolf
(verb)

______________ her and pulls her
(verb ending in -s)

to safety. As she ______________ him
(verb ending in -s)

and walks off, Wolf's ______________ begins to
(body part)

______________. It's a/n ______________ that
(verb) (noun)

Wolf has never felt before. But what is it? He

______________ it off, he has a job to
(verb ending in -s)

do! No time for thinking it over!

GOOD BAD

BAD GOOD

SOMETHING SMELLS FISHY

ADVERB ______________________

VERB ______________________

ADJECTIVE ______________________

VERB ENDING IN -ED ______________________

ADJECTIVE ______________________

FOOD ______________________

VERB ______________________

FEELING ______________________

ADJECTIVE ______________________

SOUND EFFECT ______________________

PLACE ______________________

UNIT OF TIME ______________________

ADJECTIVE ______________________

NOUN ______________________

TIP: A feeling can be something like *happy*, *sad*, or *fearful*!

Tarantula, still in the Security Room, types

________________ (adverb), trying to ________________ (verb) the security system. This would be a/n ________________ (adjective) job if she weren't being ________________ (verb ending in -ed) by the smell of ________________ (adjective) ________________ (food).

"Piranha!" Tarantula cries out. "I'm sorry! I ________________ (verb) when I get ________________ (feeling)!"

With a/n ________________ (adjective) ________________ (sound effect), all the lights in the ________________ (place) go out. When they came back on, in a/n ________________ (unit of time), the ________________ (adjective) ________________ (noun) trophy was nowhere to be seen!

MAKING A BREAK FOR IT

NOUN ____________________

ADJECTIVE ____________________

ADJECTIVE ____________________

NOUN ____________________

CLOTHING ____________________

ADVERB ____________________

ADJECTIVE ____________________

ADJECTIVE ____________________

NOUN ____________________

NOUN ____________________

VERB ENDING IN -ED ____________________

"Ladies and ____________________, please remain
(noun)

____________________," said Governor Foxington.
(adjective)

"I'm sure there's a/n ______________ explanation
(adjective)

for all of this!" Using the _________________, the
(noun)

Bad Guys slip back into their ____________ and
(clothing)

_________________________ make their way past the
(adverb)

_________________ crowd. "_________________ work,
(adjective) (adjective)

everybody," said Wolf. "Now let's make like

a/n ______________ and get the ____________ out of
(noun) (noun)

here." "Ahh, wordplay," ________________ Piranha.
(verb ending in -ed)

"I don't get it!"

THAT SPECIAL FEELING

VERB ______

VERB ENDING IN -ED ______

VERB ENDING IN -ING ______

GROUP OF PEOPLE ______

VERB ENDING IN -ING ______

ADJECTIVE ______

VERB ENDING IN -ING ______

FAVORITE ANIMALS ______

NOUN ______

FEELING ______

ADJECTIVE ______

NOUN ______

BODY PART ______

ADVERB ______

ADJECTIVE ______

"Governor Foxington, ______________ to
(verb)

me!" ______________ Professor
(verb ending in -ed)

Marmalade. "I didn't do all those things—

______________ the ______________,
(verb ending in -ing) (group of people)

______________ for the ______________ people,
(verb ending in -ing) (adjective)

and ______________ all those
(verb ending in -ing)

______________ for a/n ______________!
(favorite animals) (noun)

I did it for the ______________! For that
(feeling)

______________ ______________ I
(adjective) (noun)

get in my ______________." Wolf stopped
(body part)

______________. Why did that sound
(adverb)

______________ to him? What was
(adjective)

Professor Marmalade up to?

ANOTHER SPARK OF GOODNESS

VERB ENDING IN -ED ____________

NOUN ____________

VERB ENDING IN -ED ____________

ADJECTIVE ____________

NOUN ____________

VERB ENDING IN -ING ____________

CLOTHING ____________

VERB ____________

ADJECTIVE ____________

SOUND EFFECT ____________

EXCLAMATION ____________

NUMBER ____________

VERB ENDING IN -ED ____________

VERB ENDING IN -ING ____________

Wolf was so ________________ by Marmalade's
(verb ending in -ed)

________________ that he ________________, the
(noun) (verb ending in -ed)

________________ ________________ Trophy
(adjective) (noun)

________________ from his ________________.
(verb ending in -ing) (clothing)

It ________________ on the floor with a/n
(verb)

________________ ________________.
(adjective) (sound effect)

"________________!" shouted the police
(exclamation)

chief as ________ officers ________________ Wolf,
(number) (verb ending in -ed)

________________________ the trophy.
(verb ending in -ing)

This can't be good . . .

LOCK 'EM UP

EXCLAMATION ______________________

VERB ENDING IN -ED ______________________

VEHICLE ______________________

NOUN ______________________

VERB ______________________

CLOTHING ______________________

ADVERB ______________________

NOUN ______________________

VERB ENDING IN -ING ______________________

NOUN ______________________

"_______________________!" shouted Shark as they
(exclamation)

______________________________ him in the police
(verb ending in -ed)

__________________________ with the rest of the Bad
(vehicle)

Guys. The grappling hook __________________ that
(noun)

was supposed to ____________________________ them
(verb)

to safety had done nothing but tear Wolf's

_________________________ off. And everything had
(clothing)

been going so ___________________________! Still,
(adverb)

Snake could see the __________________________ in
(noun)

Wolf's head _____________________________. He had
(verb ending in -ing)

a/n ____________________!
(noun)

WOLF'S BIG BAD BAMBOOZLE

VERB ENDING IN -ED ______________________

NOUN ______________________

VEHICLE ______________________

VERB ______________________

VERB ENDING IN -ED ______________________

ADJECTIVE ______________________

ADJECTIVE ______________________

PLURAL NOUN ______________________

ADJECTIVE ______________________

NOUN ______________________

ADJECTIVE ______________________

VERB ______________________

Wolf ______________ his way to the
(verb ending in -ed)

______________ of the police ______________.
(noun) (vehicle)

"You know, I just want to ______________ the
(verb)

governor and police chief. You really had us

______________. We're nothing but a bunch of
(verb ending in -ed)

______________, ______________ ______________.
(adjective) (adjective) (plural noun)

It's a real shame we were never given the chance

to be anything more than ______________ criminals
(adjective)

. . . If only there was someone who could make

the ______________ of ______________ ______________ inside
(noun) (adjective) (verb)

of us . . ."

MARMALADE'S EXPERIMENT

VERB ENDING IN -ED ______________________________

PLURAL NOUN ______________________________

VERB ENDING IN -ING ______________________________

NOUN ______________________________

ADJECTIVE ______________________________

NOUN ______________________________

NOUN ______________________________

SPECIAL OCCASION ______________________________

VERB ENDING IN -ED ______________________________

VERB ______________________________

ADJECTIVE ______________________________

NOUN ______________________________

NOUN ______________________________

"Wait!" ________________ Professor Marmalade.
(verb ending in -ed)

"These ________________ may be criminals,
(plural noun)

basically ________________ ________________. But
(verb ending in -ing) (noun)

how can we say they're ________________ if
(adjective)

they've never been given a/n ________________?
(noun)

What if we tried a little ________________?
(noun)

As you know, ________________ is
(special occasion)

coming up. If I can prove to everyone there

that the Bad Guys have ________________,
(verb ending in -ed)

will you ________________ them and give
(verb)

them a/n ________________ ________________?"
(adjective) (noun)

The professor let

out a little

________________ when
(noun)

the governor agreed.

THE BIG PLAN

VEHICLE ______________________________

VERB ______________________________

VERB ENDING IN -ED ______________________________

NOUN ______________________________

ADVERB ______________________________

UNIT OF TIME ______________________________

VERB ENDING IN -ING ______________________________

VERB ENDING IN -ING ______________________________

VERB ENDING IN -ING ______________________________

FLAVOR ______________________________

VERB ______________________________

PLACE ______________________________

ADJECTIVE ______________________________

NOUN ______________________________

VERB ______________________________

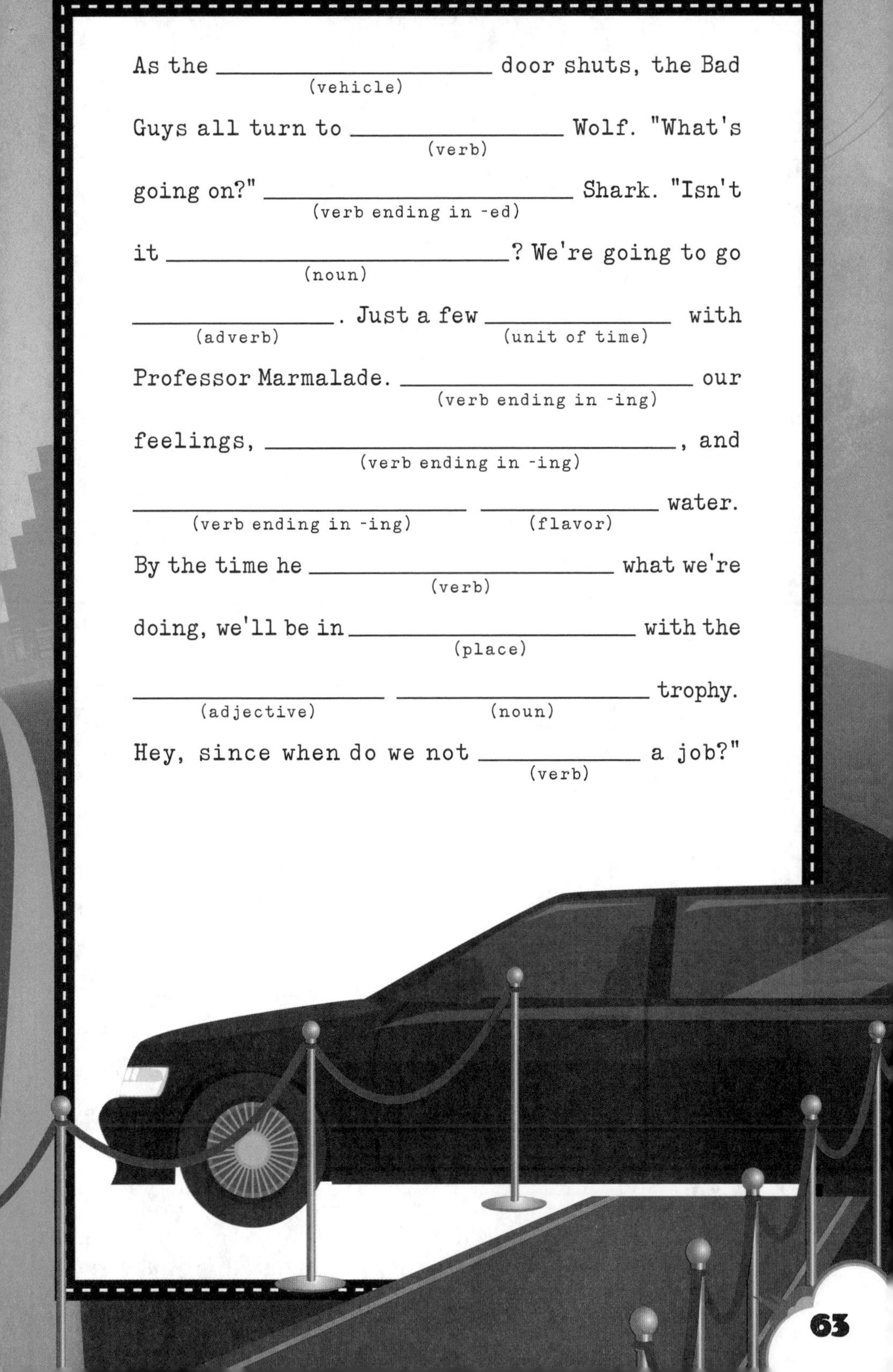

As the __________ (vehicle) door shuts, the Bad Guys all turn to __________ (verb) Wolf. "What's going on?" __________ (verb ending in -ed) Shark. "Isn't it __________ (noun)? We're going to go __________ (adverb). Just a few __________ (unit of time) with Professor Marmalade. __________ (verb ending in -ing) our feelings, __________ (verb ending in -ing), and __________ (verb ending in -ing) __________ (flavor) water. By the time he __________ (verb) what we're doing, we'll be in __________ (place) with the __________ (adjective) __________ (noun) trophy. Hey, since when do we not __________ (verb) a job?"

"NOW THAT WE'VE HAD SOME TIME TO GET ACQUAINTED . . . WE'RE NOT SO SCARY AFTER ALL!"

What makes someone a Good Guy? Cheering up their friends when they're sad? Putting other people's needs before their own? Making sacrifices so others can be happy? Maybe these guys aren't so *bad* after all.

BEING GOOD JUST FEELS SO GOOD.